I0552695

MELISSA

AGAINST THE

WORLD

MELISSA

AGAINST THE WORLD

by

KHAYAH

DANIELLA BROWNE

Melissa Against The World by Khayah
Daniella Browne

All rights reserved, including the right to
reproduce this book or portions thereof in
any for whatsoever

Published by Minds of Creation, Calabar
Nigeria
www.mindsofcreation.com
Plot 1 Ministry of Works Road, Ekorinim
2, Calabar

 Copyright 2014 Khayah Daniella Browne
1st Edition: 2014
ISBN 978-978-53275-4-0
NATIONAL Library of Nigeria

Illustrated by
Bassey.B.Inyang
Charles.C. Chukukere

DEDICATED

TO

GIRLS WITHOUT VOICES

ACKNOWLEDGEMENTS

I want to thank God for blessing me with good life experiences and wonderful parents. I thank them for not giving up on me when I was born at two pounds and they do not give up on me now. They take no excuses for why I think I can't accomplish something. I wrote the book when I was 11 years old but I am determined to make a difference and be an inspiration to others. I would also like to thank my teachers at Reading Rainbow U.S. Virgin Island and Surefoot International School Nigeria West Africa for inspiring me to challenge myself at all times

INTRODUCTION

Melissa Against the World is a book filled with mystery, suspense, and adventure. It is a book that relates my thought as I see how a young lady can be stricken with disaster and never moves on until she gets closure. For Melissa, it was the commitment to get revenge for her parent's death, and by doing so, she managed to fulfill her parents dream to eradicate the Drug Lords that were destroying the city she loved.

Contents

1. Happy Times   1
2. The Secret Room   7
3. Drug Trouble   14
4. Revenge of the Drug Lords   21
5. The Safe House   29
6. Melissa Finds a Friend   36
7. Melissa Gets Serious   44
8. Return of Uncle Frank   50
9. The Plot   58
10. Sweet Revenge   68

Biographical Notes

Melissa remembers happy times with her family

Chapter 1

HAPPY TIMES

"I never thought the world would be so cruel to me" said Melissa. Melissa was only eight, and her brother Jack was 14 years old when her parents died. When she found out that it was a murder, she promised herself that she would not spare her parents' killers.

Her parents were Johnny and Margaret, and she loved them more than words could express. Her father was a police officer and her mother a detective. They worked long hours together each day fighting crime in Arizona State where she was born.

Her mother used to tell her "Life was beautiful when I was your age. All the children on our block ran up and down the street playing, and we never locked our doors. Our parents did not have to worry about anything happening to us."

"Why have things changed mom?" Melissa would ask

"Drugs and crime came in and destroyed our beautiful state, and it has never been the same," she said with disappointment in her eyes as she looked at Melissa.

"This is why we work so hard my dear, to make this place safe for all of us to live without fear." She would say as she kissed me on the cheek.

"I love you, my dear, see you later," she said as she walked off towards the door.

"See you later Precious, love you too." Daddy would say as they both rushed out the door.

Her mother loved making stories and singing to Melissa and Jack. When they were small, mom used to read all kinds of wonderful stories. Her mother was gorgeous and funny, and whenever anyone needed a good joke to cheer them up, they called on her. She had long brown hair and a great smile that everyone loved. She was an excellent detective that dealt with anything or anyone that was in her way and anyone that came between her, and her family. She came up with the most outrageous fighting moves that no one could handle.

Her father, Johnny was very handsome, he was creative too. In his free time, he would write beautiful poems which he would read to Margaret. He had black hair like Jack and brown eyes just like Margaret. Johnny was the head police officer of the Police Precinct. He once headed his police precinct to battle against the Gangs of Chicago before they got married.

My brother Jack was 14 and was very creative. He would imagine his world and run around discovering his imaginary things with his best friend Simon who also lived in the neighborhood. Jack was also an excellent painter. His dream was to be the most famous artist in the world.

Melissa always remembered those days fondly, because she knew her parents were working hard to make them happy.

Their hours of work were so long at times that Melissa had to go to her Uncle's house to stay while they did what they had to do. Melissa understood that her parents had an outstanding job, so she did not fuss when they had to go sometimes for days because Uncle Frank made everything better. One day mom said that a long time ago Uncle Frank had a bad past and could not be trusted. But, those days were long gone because he is doing the right thing now.

Uncle Frank was her favorite uncle who lived two doors from where they lived. Her memories of him were the most exciting times she had in her life. Uncle Frank was a funny man who was serious and was another person everyone looked to for entertainment. He made some of the most hilarious jokes while keeping his face very serious; those made everyone laugh hysterically. His stories were fascinating and kept everyone glued to their seats wanting more and more.

He would ask "Do you know how many times I cheated death?

"No Frank," everyone would say while they made themselves comfortable in a chair to listen to his story of the day.

"No one knows when death will come, but it is up to us to run like hell if you see it coming." He would say with a serious face.

"Hey Mom, can I get a...?" was all I could say before Mom brushed me off to the side.

"Hush child, Uncle Frank is about to tell us one of his tall tales." She would say as she sat waiting eagerly listening to his every word.

"I sat patiently waiting on the man they called "The Ghost." No one knew who he was, or even saw his face." Frank said mysteriously.

"He would give a call and told to meet him somewhere, but he would never say what day." He looked up and sighed. "One day he asked me to meet him at Duke Street by Vini's Café in the corner by the big fridge. It was so dark in that neighborhood; people called it the "Dark Zone," he said in an eerie voice that made me shiver.

I waited in the Dark Zone at 8 pm for three days before "The Ghost" appeared dressed all in black from his head to toe: hat, sunglasses, coat, and shoe.

"Let's go!" he said. I followed him out the door and around the corner where I saw a suspicious black car parked in the alleyway.

We passed the black car which I looked at carefully, to run if anything was to happen suddenly.

With a jerk of my hand "The Ghost "pulled me inside the car and told the driver, "Let's Go!."

"The car was totally dark with just him, me, and the driver made three. I was afraid only because anything could go wrong at any time, so I waited for his next move." Frank said touching his chin.

"We need to take care of "The Boss" in El-Salvador. He is becoming a huge problem for the government, and they want him dead," said "The Ghost."

"I have to go," Melissa would say as she ran to her room too scared to listen to what came next. I would hug my favorite bear and sing songs to make sure I did not hear.

Before Uncle Frank left for his home, he would make sure that he came and gave me a kiss and say, "I was just telling stories my child. I hope I did not scare you too much."

"Yes you did, but I still love you." Melissa would say. With a big hug and several more kisses, he would give me a hug good night as he tucked me into bed.

If Uncle Frank was not telling scary stories to us at home, he was entertaining me at his home with cookies and ice cream, my favorite food.

Those were some of the happiest days I could

remember because they had funny stories, and yes ice cream. Family get-togethers were every month, as a rule, no particular day, but every month.

My parents loved each other so much, if they were not at work, they were hugging all the time especially when they were watching TV. That was not too often, but as often as they could. I would see them kiss, and I would remember saying "Stop that!" while I covered my eyes not to see.

"We love each other, and this is what grown folks do when they are in love." Dad would say kissing me on the cheek.

My brother was too busy with either school or his friends to bother with me. At times, he would run in and out the house with his best friend, Simon.

"Where are you going?" I would ask.

"None of your business," he would reply patting me on my head.

I loved my brother so much, but I wished he would invite me to hang out with him and Simon sometimes. Well, Uncle Frank made up for all the times I did not see mom, dad, or Jack.

And so she remembers the happy times she spent with her mother, father, Jack, and of course Uncle Frank, who was her most favorite person in the world.

Chapter 2

THE SECRET ROOM

I was twelve when I was at Uncle Frank's house as usual. Mom and Dad were out to work, and I was in my particular room feeling a little bored, not knowing what to do. I looked at the guitar Uncle Frank bought me, but I did not want to play anything that day. This time of the day was his quiet time when I did not bother him because he had work to do. I got some milk and cookies and curled up in front of the TV watching my favorite show.

TV time was over now, but I was still up and restless trying to find something to do. I decided to go downstairs into the library to get a good book to read. Uncle Frank had a special section in the library just for me. It had the most beautiful books and movies I could see and understand. I looked through the stack to see if he got me any new stuff from his last trip. I knew

Melissa watching her Uncle Frank practicing his
fighting in his secret room

that sometimes he would hide them in another section to keep them as a surprise so off I went in search to see if I had any surprises hidden.

I looked and looked but no surprise. I then decided to see if any of Uncle Frank's books would peek my curiosity. I got down one that said "The art of Kung-fu." It had many wonderful pictures, and some great moves I decided to try. I laughed at myself because I knew that I looked silly. I placed that book back and decided to look for another one.

As I pulled out that particular book, I noticed that I could see directly into an empty room. I was surprised because I never knew that anything was in this chamber but books, a desk, and a chair. I kept looking into the room wondering what was there. Just then Uncle Frank called my name.

"Melissa, Melissa, where are you Precious?" That was my other name he would say.

"I am reading in the library," I said as I placed back the book rapidly.

"I was worried that you left me here all alone to bore myself," he said as he smiled.

"I could not sleep, so I came for a good book to read."

"Here is a good one." He pulled out a new one from the very top of my side of the shelf.

"Uncle Frank!!!" I said frantically looking down at the book and beginning to read.

Uncle Frank picked me up in his big arms and said, "Off to bed now, and you can continue reading another day." And to bed he took me.

"Good night, sleep tight; don't let the alligators catch you." He said with a smile.

"Good night Uncle Frank, even though that made absolute no sense I still love you," I stated with a big grin and drifted off to bed remembering that secret room I saw and wondering what was in there.

The next day I came from school and went to Uncle Frank's house as planned. It was night time now, and it was his quiet time as usual. I still remembered that particular room I saw in the back of the bookshelf, so I went downstairs in search of the secret room.

Uncle Frank had two hours of quiet time when I could not disturb him while he worked. I never saw him during those two hours, so that was the perfect time to go in search of the secret room.

I pulled out the book again and looked inside the chamber. "Where could the entrance be?" I said to myself softly while looking everywhere I could, but no opening was present except the door I came through. So, back to the bookshelf, I went pulling out more books to see if I could climb into the room from there. I pulled the books from side to side but no room. I pulled the books directly to the top and the one at the bottom, but no room. Just then I looked up and saw a funny little book that peeked my interest.

Too high for me to reach so I took a chair, stood up on top and reached balancing on my tippy toes. I pulled it and to my surprise, the wall at the side opened just a crack for me to get inside. "Wow!" I exclaimed silently. I jumped down, ran to the library door and locked it so no one could see what I contemplated.

I walked inside the once hidden doorway slowly, and carefully; not sure what I would find. "This could be the greatest mystery, what a find." Rubbing my hands together and smiling evilly.

I was now in a hallway leading to a door to the far end of the secret door. I crept slowly to the room and opened it just a crack. To my surprise, I saw Uncle Frank sitting in front of a TV listening to a man speak.

I was amazed, astonished, and excited to see such strange things in that room. I saw a wall with weapons at one end, then an area with some people standing still, then a white area with a light shining on the spot, and nothing else.

I looked back at Uncle Frank, who was listening intensely. I now began to see if I could make out what the man on the TV screen was saying. "It's time to start your training for this mission, so, I will walk you through every step as you go. Let's begin." Uncle Frank got up and started to follow the instructions.

What I witnessed was amazing. Uncle Frank

11

was doing things I have never seen before in real life. After an hour he stopped and fell into the big chair while he listened to the TV again. I heard fantastic information of secrets, espionage, and treasonous crimes of great men of power. My uncle was instructed with accurate information directing him to places and doing things I did not understand. He was instructed to go to his virtual wall to see the layout of his next project. Then, to my amazement things came alive, buildings appeared, doors opened people started to walk in every direction all around my uncle: all of this happened on the spot where that bright light was shining. I saw people appear from nowhere. They were not real, but they were there.

"How is this possible? "WOW!!!" I exclaimed quietly. As if my uncle was about to turn in my direction; I quickly faded back into the library, closed the secret door, then I ran to my room falling onto my bed exhausted and still excited with what I witnessed. "That was incredible!!!" I said excitedly jumping to my feet doing kicks, and spins and turns falling into a heap as I fell from my awkward display of Karate. I could not contain myself from that moment and could not wait to visit my uncle's home more often to learn all I had seen and heard from that very secret place my uncle had hidden behind the bookshelf.

Meanwhile, my parents were working on the biggest drug bust of a lifetime. The operation took time away from the two most important people in their lives: their children, but it was worth it if they could make the town safe for them to live.

They would bring presents for me and Jack when they return home from their training sessions. These presents made me thrilled and excited to see them because the gifts were. ??

Lives lost because of drugs

Chapter 3

DRUG TROUBLE

It is morning time now, and the Gonzalez Crime Family were busy planning to receive their new drug shipment. All information about the location, time, and exact date of arrival was top secret. This was the biggest drug delivery that year and everything must go smoothly because millions of dollars were at stake.

The police and CIA were also interested in the activities of the crime family because too many lives were being lost from drug crimes in the city. The word was out about the drugs arrival amongst law enforcement, but no one knew the details, not even Julio had any information for them after being inside for two years. Julio was the best informant they had in a long time. All of his leads led to arrests and many convictions. No one in the Gonzalez Crime Family ever suspected him because of his unwavering loyalty.

"Julio, you have been one of our strongest brothers and a good amigo to me. Tonight, I want you to supervise this most important shipment coming in at Beon's Bay," said Papa, the head of the Gonzalez, crime family.

"Yes Papa, but why is this delivery so different from all the other transfers we've handled in the past?" asked Julio.

"This shipment will bring in 100 million, and that is much more than we have ever brought into the country at one time. This drug is pure and stronger than any we ever had."

"This is good news, and our customers will love it. Our young sellers will make a fortune," Julio said with conviction and admiration in his voice

"Come with me; let us make sure that all the details are tight because we don't want mistakes tonight. We have one hour to get ready for its arrival."

"One hour, wow, that is close. We have no time to waste so let me know what you expect from me." They headed off to the door. Julio now was worried that he did not have enough time to warn his captain and the CIA of this shipment, but he had to find a way.

The men went about for the next 15 minutes securing all information, making sure that the delivery was being tracked, and the contact at the port was in the position to receive the shipment.

"All is secure on all the ends, and the shipment is ready for pickup," Julio said

Get yourself in position at the port and

prepare to collect the delivery. Franco will be your contact person at the dock. I am counting on you." Papa directed him to exit at their escape route.

As he proceeded towards the awaiting vehicle, he made an emergency 30315 to the commander's untraceable line. That message meant that the operation would be in 30mins at Pier 315. Once the message was sent, he deleted it and continued to the awaiting vehicle

"Let's go; we have no time to waste." He said to the driver as they moved away from the building.

On the way to the port, Julio's heart raced because he was not sure if the captain got his message. He prayed that he would have a backup in place, but worried that 30 minutes was too short notice to get things together for such a large operation. At this point, all he could do is pray for the best.

At the dock, he met Franco, who was a strong man in his mid-30s. The two men greeted each other and waited with ten other bodyguards and drug lords at strategic locations. This was a standard formation and best suited to avoid drawing attention to what was going on.

Time went by slowly, tick, tock, tick, tock, tick tock as each second seem like a lifetime. Preparing for battle, anticipating each person's move, making sure he knew where every man was at all times. It was now 15 minutes for the show and no suspicious movements, no sign of his undercover partners getting in position, nothing. Just dead silence, the kind that makes the hardest man think about his future. These were the crucial moments when most men make mistakes.

At the police station, 30315 messages were received by the Police Chief and the CIA officers. "All hands on deck, the sting operation is going down tonight in 30 minutes. We need all available officers to be at the port at dock 315. Officer Juan is on point and needs our assistance,"

Officers went running in all directions: ammunition room, dressing in bulletproof vests, briefings, helmets, and out the door, they went. "The CIA was notified so all will convene at Dock 315 for further instructions." shouted the Police Chief.

A call was placed to Officer Romano, who was a plain clothes officer in the shipping industry to see his location. Luckily for us he was on board the cargo ship, right in the proper place for our sting operation.

The cargo ship was in sight approaching slowly. Everyone was perched waiting with anticipation. All of a sudden Papa pulled up in a Cadillac. He stepped out wearing one of his finest suits cradling a machine gun in his jacket. "Everything OK, mis hermanos?" he asked.

"Everything is just fine, and all is on schedule with no disruptions to report," Julio said with authority in his voice.

"Now we wait, things look good so far but prepare for action at any time. Every so often those pigs come down on us. We have a snitch, and we will flush him out eventually." said Papa angrily.

"That kind of dishonesty should never be permitted in this family. When we catch him, he'll know what it means to be loyal." Julio was clenching at his gun in disgust, but sweating inside his shirt knowing that things can go crazy in a minute and that he might have to kill the man he called Papa.

One flash came from the ship, and one returned from the dock signaling that all contacts were on point and shipment was in place.

"How come you are here tonight? This is an operation for your sons to do." Said Julio to Papa

"This is my operation, and I want to know who is messing with my property. I am prepared to kill them all." Papa whispered under his breath.

"You said you wanted me to be in charge of the operation tonight. I am just surprised to see you here. I don't think that we will have any trouble, things are moving quite smoothly." The giant door of the cargo ship opened, and movement began in all directions. Containers were driving out, and some were being lifted from the top of the ship. I wondered which one was ours.

Our contact signaled to us that our container was on its way out, so we braced for action. I prayed that my message to the Police Chief went through, and everyone was in position for action.

Chapter 4

REVENGE OF THE DRUG LORDS

It's been two days now, and things have settled down a little in the police precincts. The media was buzzing at the huge success of the recent drug bust of the Gonzales Drug Cartel; the biggest shipment in the past twenty years was stopped dead in its track. Thousands of lives saved from the seizure of this load of nearly 3,500 pounds of cocaine with a street value more than $250 million. They predicted that they were on high alert because of the death of Juan Carlos Renaldo Gonzales, the son of Pablo Gonzalez the head drug lord who had vowed revenge for his son's death.

The police knew they would feel the impact of killing the son of Pablo. However, no one knew what was going to take place in the days that followed, but everyone was preparing for the worse. Criminal activities started to escalate:

Once Papa's son died no one was safe again
from the Gonzales family

drive-byes, murders execution style, assaults on police officers, and several hangings of law enforcement officers and their families.

"Things are going to get worse before they get better," said the Police Chief to his officers.

"We knew that this bust would be big, and we knew that people would die. The death of Papa's son was a big blow to the Gonzalez family," said Melissa's dad Johnny.
"We need to keep alert, and watch out for each other," said Margaret cautioning the officers.

"Papa Gonzales is mad, and he will not think twice to kill us all. In fact, we are all on his hit list," she said again.

"For the next month, we will be patrolling all the neighborhoods looking for any suspicious activities." The police chief said.

In the dead of the night, they came in a car, four in all: two stayed outside the house and two entered from the rear. They climbed through the window of the bedroom and rushing at Melissa's parents dragging them from the bed. Wide awake now they were pressed up against the wall and begging for their lives.

"Don't hurt us," said mom while another man threw Johnny unto the ground pushing his foot into his back. "Please don't hurt him," Margaret begged for her husband.

"Shut up!!!" One of the intruders said hitting Margaret on her face with the gun.

Melissa was not at home. However, her brother woke up to a loud disturbance happening in his parent's room. To his horror, he saw his mother pushed up against a wall with guns in her face. He saw his father on the floor with the other man on top of him.

Sizing up the situation, he escaped without being seen and called the police. Lucky for him the police were already patrolling the area, so they came rushing over and into the house. Sensing that the police had arrived Jack hid in his room waiting for the next sound.

"BANG, BANG, BANG, BANG!!!" screaming, then silence. The gunshots came from his parent's room. Jack feared the worse, so he rushed out the room right into the face of one of the intruders.

"I will be back to get you, let them know this is for Papas, son!" the thief shouted as he rushed out the door colliding into the police officers entering the room. At that exact moment, a car came from around the corner speeding and firing bullets in every direction.

"Officer down," shouted an officer after the gun firing stopped. "Calling for backup, and calling for the ambulance," he yelled again as he entered the house to protect Officer Johnny and Detective Margaret Smith.

They rushed into the bedroom and realized that they were too late. Jack rushed in behind them and to his horror, he saw his parents on the floor. They just lay lifeless.

"Mom, Dad, wake up, wake up," he shook them sobbing knowing that they were gone. "Mom, Dad, don't leave me here all alone, I need you, please don't leave me all alone," pressing his face into his mother's chest. Sobbing and sobbing, until one of the officers took him away from the room.

"We are here for you, we love your parents and are here for you," comforting Jack

"I want my parents, why did this happen?" he continued sobbing.

The house came alive with officers all around, asking questions to each other, calling on the phone to the captain. Everyone was sad now knowing that this was something personal.

"Did you see them, did they see you?" one officer asked.

"Yes, they saw me.", Jack cried worried at the thought.

"Did they say anything to you?" the officer asked.

"Yes, one man said let them know that this is for Papa, but I don't know what that means," Jack said confused and shook.

"I am Officer Davis, where is your sister?" one female officer asked.

"She is at my uncle's house two houses down the street," Jack muttered still sobbing.

"Come with me, we will get your sister and go to see Captain Simpson," Officer Davis said.
Jack was whisked downstairs into a police car. As they moved off, they stopped to pick up Melissa. They knocked on the door, and Melissa looked out. She saw Jack in the distance looking from the backseat of the police car. She looked at the officer's face and their uniforms and opened the door.

"Are you Melissa?' asked Officer Davis.

"Yes I am," answered Melissa a little confused.

"Something happened at your home, and you need to come with us right now." Officer Davis suggested with urgency.

"What is going on Jack?" Melissa locked the door and walked to the car. She looked at Jack tear stained face and knew that something terrible was wrong.

"What's wrong Jack?" she asked, "Where is Mom and Dad, where are they taking us?"

"They are dead. Some men came and shot them," said Jack as he began to sob again now holding Melissa while she shook her head in disbelief trying not to cry.

"What will we do? Who will take care of us? Uncle Frank is out of town and I don't know how to reach him," Melissa said as she finally gave in and started crying.

"I don't know Melissa. I don't know," he said worriedly now but trying to protect his little sister.

In the police station, officers hugged the children expressing their sorrows Officer Davis and other officers took the children to Chief Simson's room.

"Sit down children. Much has happened tonight. Your parents will not be coming back," he said as a tear rolled down his cheek.
The children knew that this was serious and that they would never see their parents again.

"What will happen to us?" asked Melissa.

"The intruders were from the Gonzales drug family, and they saw Jack, so you are not safe here. We will have to take you to a safe house far away while we sort things out here."

"What about Uncle Frank? How will he find us?" Melissa asked.

"We will let him know but now you need to be safe. Officer Davis will take you to the safe house and stay with you," the Chief said.
The children hugged each other as they left the police station not sure what they would do. "I will take care of you, Melissa," Jack said as they entered the cop's car.

They took them to the airport and flew them away to a place the children never saw before.

"Where are we? What about school?" Melissa asked Officer Davis.
They arrived at a safe house, and the officers directed them to their rooms. Melissa sat on Jack's bed too afraid to leave him.

"One day I will make them pay for this. They are dangerous people," said Melissa to Jack

"They stated that it was for Papa. I don't know who Papa is but he is a Drug Lord. Why did they have to kill our parents?" the children began crying as they fell asleep exhausted from the events of the day.

Chapter 5

THE SAFE HOUSE

It was morning time now, and the children were now stirring after a long tiring night.

"Melissa, Melissa, wake up," Jack shook Melissa as he looked around to see where he was and remembered what had happened.

"Stop, stop that Jack!" Melissa muttered angrily under her voice. She opened her eyes and looked at the room. "Where are we?"

"We were brought here last night after mom and dad got hurt, remember."
She shook her head and feelings of sadness filled her heart "Yes I remember."

"What is going to happen to us now?"

"I don't know, but we will find out soon."
Just then Officer Davis knocked on the door and entered. "Remember me; I am Officer Davis from the precinct. I brought you here last night, do you remember?"

"Yes," Jack replied, "What is going to happen

Secret Information Sold to Drug Lords

30

to us, and where are we

"We had to bring you here for your protection. Some dangerous people hurt your parents, and they might want to hurt you."

"But why? We did nothing wrong." Melissa began to cry as she put her head on Jack's lap.

"You are safe here," as she touched Melissa's hair affectionately. "Jack, did you see the men who hurt your parents? Did they see you?"

"Yes, I saw them when I ran out of my bedroom door. The man said that he would be back to get me and to let them know this is for Papa's son." Jack said now getting angry as he remembered what happened.

"Who was that man, why did he kill our parents, why did he want to come back and get me?"

"The evil man knows that you can identify him. Your parents were very special to us; we had to make sure that you were safe, so we brought you here."

"Why do they want to hurt us? We didn't do anything wrong." Melissa said sadly.

"I know. Your parents tried to make life safe for us all and we loved them dearly," she paused with sadness in her eyes. "Jack do you remember what the men look like?"

"Yes, I can't ever forget their faces."

"I will have one of our officers come and take a sketch from you this evening so we can arrest those men that hurt your parents."

That night Jack gave his description to the artist.

Meanwhile at home Papa was angry at his men for leaving a witness alive.

"You have to find the child and get rid of him. He can identify you," Papa snapped "Get our informant in the police department. Get his location and get rid of him once and for all!"

"AN EYE FOR AN EYE! They killed my son and they will all pay!!!" Papa screamed as his men went running to find the missing child.

Back at the Safe House, the children had many questions about what was going to happen to them with no parents to take care of them.

"Who will take care of us now? Where will we go to school? Who will we play with? Where is Uncle Frank?" Melissa had many questions for Officer Davis, who tried her best to answer them all.

"I will be with you from now on. You can't go to school for now, but we will provide you with your school books and a tutor so you can keep up with school, and your Uncle Frank will be informed," the officer replied.

"I am very sad. I want my mom and dad to come and get me now!" Melissa began to shout on the verge of crying again as she tried to make sense of what was going on.

Jack took a closer look at Officer Davis as she spoke to them. She was a tall, slim woman, with brown hair, big eyes, and a small mouth but she was pretty. She could not replace his parents nor would he let her. He looked at her angrily.

"Are you hungry? We have cereal, milk, bread, eggs, and cheese in the fridge for breakfast." Officer Davis said changing the subject.

"Yes, I am?" Melissa snapped as she got off the bed and followed the Officer downstairs. Jack followed closely behind making sure that things were safe for Melissa because he was her big brother and she needed her protection now.

The investigation was ongoing and two years had passed. Melissa was now ten years old and her world was about to be turned upside down again.

Revealed, snitched on, found out. They were awakened by gunshots. Jack immediately got Melissa to the closet.

"Melissa, hide here. If anything happens, you run, run and never look back," he grabbed a stack of money from the draw that Officer Davis gave them for an emergency. "I love you," he kissed Melissa placing the money and her emergency bag in her hands then he ran out the room to make sure they did not find her.

Melissa heard more gun firing and then silence. Then next thing she knew, smoke was filling the room, and she was still inside. So, she quickly got out of the closet and made her way to the window. She looked all around, but no one was there; only a car was speeding off in the distance. She remembered all the beautiful things she learned at her Uncle's house and all the days and nights she and Jack spent fighting, and training in the Safe House, if anything was to happen to them. She got out of the house and ran as fast as she could.

She stopped and waited for Jack. In the distance she could see the house burning, the fire truck was extinguishing the flames, but Jack never came out.

She stood from a safe distance and waited but still no Jack, by then she had realized that Jack was gone. She was now all alone, and she had to survive, she knew that the drug lords were burning down their new home. No one must know that I am alive, but they will pay for what they did to my parents.

"I will make them pay for destroying my family!!!" she shouted as she ran to safety more determined than ever to get revenge on the killers of her family and Papa was the main suspect.

That fateful day she changed. She never spoke again. Melissa became depressed because now she was living on the streets 100 miles from the safe house trying to make her way back to Uncle Frank. Melissa hated life. She sat back and thought about killing herself because there was no purpose to life. Her brother, father, and mother were now all gone. All the money her brother gave her was now gone, and she had to find ways for herself to survive.

Melissa meets Samantha

Chapter 6

MELISSA FINDS A FRIEND

It was time for Melissa to get to work. She got a little job bagging groceries at Sam and Jan Supermarket. It was not much, but it was manageable. She continued hustling on the streets to save up enough money to buy a guitar and to get back home to Uncle Frank's house.

Melissa never went to school again but she was very smart. She had learned to sing from her mother and learned to play the guitar from Uncle Frank. Melissa loved playing guitar and singing on the streets because she made extra money that way.

She grew angrier every day and had to keep focused on keeping her promise that she wouldn't stop until that promise was fulfilled to revenge the killing of her family.

Another day came, and it was time again for her to go to work. The day was long and hard and full of drama as usual. When she was going back to her place, a big man grabbed her from behind and threw her to the wall.

"What are you doing? Don't hurt me! HELP!!! HELP!!!" she shouted, but no one was in sight to hear her cries.

With lightning speed, the man placed one hand on Melissa's mouth to silence her. "Be quiet" he growled as he grabbed her bag with his other hand.

Melissa knew at that very moment that she had to fight for her life. She hit him hard in his chest with her fist, again and again into his chest. "Leave me alone!!!" she shouted angrily. With no more time to think she dug her nails into his chest right into his shirt. She could hear the material ripping beneath her fingers as her nails dug into his flesh.

"AHHHHHH" the stranger cried in pain. In a split second he pulled her hands down from his chest. Clenching his fist, he threw it forward towards Melissa's face with a force that knocked her backward and onto the floor.

Melissa gasped for breath as the wind got knocked out of her. She screamed in pain. Melissa regained her composure fast and sprang to her feet sidestepped the stranger with surprising speed, blocking his violent attack, and countering with a brutal kick to his head.

The man fell back and looked at her with surprise. He lunged at her once again still determined to get Melissa's money, so he continued to fight her. "Stop moving! Give me all your money!" he shouted at her.

Melissa was determined not to let him win, so she continued to fight this six-foot tall stranger who was much stronger and bigger than her. He made his hand into a fist again and attacked her. With her back against the wall and nowhere to run to, she threw herself to the floor and sliding through his legs dodged his attack once again.

With no time to spare, Melissa remembered that she had a taser in her bag that she had bought from the pawn shop. She reached into her bag and took it out. The weapon fell to the floor right next to the man. She looked at the weapon and looked at him. He moved towards the taser and she knew at that time she was in trouble. Desperate now, she threw herself to the floor reaching the weapon first, knowing that the weapon she bought for protection could take her life. The man threw himself onto her to take the weapon, but Melissa did not give up the fight. She got control of the situation and tasered the man once, and his entire weight pinned her to the floor.

Terrified and alone with no one to turn to she mustered all her strength and pushed the man off and away from her as she yelled: "Get off me!"

Thinking that this fight was all over, Melissa paused for a minute to catch her breath moving off slowly.

The stranger moved like a monster in a bad movie and woke up grabbing Melissa's leg as she tried to leave. Her fear changed to anger, frustration and outrage that bad things kept happening to her. She turned around abruptly, bent down and tased the man three more times; one after the other. She tugged her foot from between the grips of his hand and took off running until she was got home.

Now in the quiet of her room, she sobbed silently about her misfortune but was strengthened by her triumph over the stranger who wanted to violate her. She won and that made her strong and more determined to accomplish the task she had on hand.

Since the day she lost her parents, her life changed forever. Melissa started to have these terrible dreams so she went to work to find something to help her with them. They began to turn into visions and it became a problem for her because she remembered Jack and her parents.

One day she was sitting all alone thinking about her mother and all the conversations they used to have about school; about her staying away from drugs, and boys. She smiled for a moment and shook herself out of her moment because she knew that it would not bring back her mother. She had to fight the urge to cry at that very moment. Instead, she tried to concentrate on the matter at hand, getting revenge for her parents and brother's death.

The next day Melissa decided to take the day off and work hustling on the street to get some more money. When she went on the street to make her music, someone took her spot. Melissa told her to get lost, and she did.

"Who are you and what are you doing on my spot!" Melissa shouted angrily.

After a while, Melissa felt bad, so she went and apologized to the girl saying "I am very sorry for yelling at you. I have been having an awful week." Melissa noticed that she had a bruise, so she hesitated while the girl continued crying. Melissa asked the girl "What happened, are you all right?"

"Nothing," she answered

Then Melissa got an idea and said "Why don't we introduce ourselves. What's your name?" asked Melissa

"Samantha."

Well, then Samantha tell me about yourself.

"Well, my parents died when I was only a baby. They had a dispute with a drug gang, and they had a car chase which ended with my parents perishing. I'm an only child; I ran away from my foster home, and I'm looking for their killers."

"Wow, that is a lot," Melissa said.

I'm not having any luck, and I don't have a place to stay," said Samantha.

"I'm just like you. The Gonzales Crime Family killed my parents. My brother and I remained in a Safe House. Two years later we were discovered, and the Safe House was burned down. My brother made sure that I was safe, but he got stuck inside and died. I am furious and plan to avenge their death. "Melissa snapped.

The girls' stories were incredible; the girls had more in common than they knew!!! Melissa asked Samantha "Where are you from?"

"Arizona," Samantha said.

"I am also from Arizona so that we might be after the same drug gang," Melissa said amazed that they shared so much in common.

"Do you want to work with me?"

"I don't know," Samantha said.

"We have a lot in common. Think about it. We can help each other to find our parents' killers and I have a place in Arizona for both of us to stay," Melissa encouraged "We can share our money and then we can get anything we want. We are the same, so I think that we can be good friends."

"I'll think about it, let's talk again tomorrow," Samantha said as she walked off.

That night when she was sleeping she had more terrible nightmares. The next day Melissa went to Samantha and Samantha accepted her proposal. They started to live and work together. Three months went by, and the girls saved enough money to buy bus tickets and disguises as they made their way to Arizona to get to Uncle Frank, learn everything they needed to know to avenge their parents' deaths.

Melissa becomes focused to accomplish her mission

Chapter 7

MELISSA GETS SERIOUS

Melissa and Samantha dressed in disguises made their way back to Uncle Frank's house. Because she had Samantha with her, she used the doorbell. She kept ringing the bell several times without any response. Uncle Frank was nowhere. Melissa looked around everywhere to make sure that no one was looking at them.

"Samantha wait here for me. Let me see if my Uncle is out back." She slipped to the back into their secret entrance then opened the door for Samantha.

"Come in Samantha. My uncle is not around but we can wait for him until he gets home."

Samantha looked around the house and was very impressed with what she saw. "This is very nice. I love it and it is better than living on the streets."

"We don't have time to get excited about Uncle Frank's house. We have work to do in Arizona and get back out." Melissa said

That night they relaxed while Melissa tried to

reach her Uncle Frank but she couldn't. She had to be careful not to make too many calls for anyone to get suspicious of their activities.

It was morning time now and no Uncle Frank so Melissa made her way to the secret room before Samantha was awake. She had to come up with a plan how to maintain the privacy of her uncle's secret too.

As Samantha ate her breakfast, Melissa briefed her on Uncle Frank's house. Melissa slipped into the library, opened the door and then called Samantha. Samantha entered the library and opened the secret entrance that Melissa had decorated to look like an ordinary doorway. She led Samantha to the door entering the secret room and waited for her reaction.

"OH MY GOD, OMG!!! Where in the world are we and what are we doing here? Is this a gym or a war zone?" the questions kept coming.
"This will be our training room until we are ready to go to battle the Drug Lords." She took her hands to close Samantha's opened mouth. Melissa mapped a training plan for the next coming months as they got prepared to go to battle.

Because Melissa was familiar with all the equipment, she guided Samantha to the exercise station to strengthen her, while practicing simple combat moves. This training lasted for two weeks until Melissa was comfortable that Samantha was ready to go on to more serious training.

They trained as hard as they could leaving the house in disguise only when they were in an absolute emergency for food supplies. They had so much to learn from the resources they had in her uncle's secret room.

Next step was training in martial arts. Melissa turned on the instructional video and they began intensive training from day to day.

"Melissa, I did not expect to be training so hard. This training facility is fabulous! I am truly impressed. And what does your uncle do? Is he a CIA agent? And is he on a secret mission?"

"No to all of your questions! My family is in law enforcement and my Uncle just believes in doing things in the extreme," Melissa said with a smile as she explained her love for her Uncle Frank.

"This is truly unbelievable and just incredible. Each day I wake to see another special day and to think we were just living on the streets. I knew what I wanted to do but had no idea how it was ever going to happen," Samantha said with tears in her eyes.

"Thank you, Melissa."

"Don't start that crying in here. We have work to do!" The girls smiled as they continued their training for the most difficult job they had ever done and it might be their last one alive.

One week later when Melissa thought they

were ready to take on fighting others in Martial Arts, Melissa turned on the virtual reality world and people appeared from everywhere. Samantha jumped with surprise as people surrounded her with weapons of every kind.

"What in the world is this, are they real?" She said amazed, confused, thrilled, and excited all at the same time.

"What is the plan, Melissa? What am I going to do with them? What? What? What? These images are amazing!!!!

"Slow down Samantha," Melissa began to laugh. "This is a virtual world where we can practice some of the techniques we learned, and it will teach us some new ones as we encounter different challenges."

"What we need to do is access the police station and try to find the records of both of our parents' cases and see how they are linked and take the drug lords down," said Melissa.
Immediately, Melissa remembered that she had stumbled upon the design of the area police station that contained the evidence of her parent's case. She always thought this could be vital information. She needed to make those murderers pay for what they did to her family.

"Let us pause for a moment so we can look at the layout of the police precinct and map out a plan to get inside and get the records we need."

Right then, like before, Melissa pressed a

button and the exact layout of the police precinct came alive. "Right here on the screen, we have the work schedule of the officers, the shift changes, the movements of cleaners, night patrol officers, and all the surveillance cameras in the building."

"How did your Uncle get this stuff? Is he a CIA agent?"

"No silly, I told you that he is in law enforcement and is a freak for details. He collects things that no one ever thinks about."

"So where exactly is your Uncle Frank? We have been here for two months now, and he has not shown up as yet," throwing her hands in the air. "I would like to meet your Uncle Frank one day; all this is amazing."

The girls continued to study the layout of the precinct and continued with training in the virtual battle zone. They were getting better and better every day and were getting closer to achieving their goal of taking revenge on the Gonzalez crime family for killing their parents.

Uncle Frank on his way home from a
secret mission

Chapter 8

RETURN OF UNCLE FRANK

As time went by the ladies continued aggressive training because the mission ahead was not only dangerous it could cost them their lives. They had to do everything possible to make sure they succeed in this mission.

One day while they were having breakfast the doorknob started to turn. The girls sprang into action because for three months now they were all alone. Only one person could be turning the key in the door, and that should be Uncle Frank. But the last time she saw Uncle Frank she was just about eight years old. Would Uncle Frank recognize her all grown up now? Would he think that they were intruders? How would they explain why they were in his house when he saw them? So many questions and no time to think when the door opened and a figure stepped in. She hoped it was Uncle Frank because all she could see was a figure in the glare of the sun. He entered cautiously already sensing that he was not alone. Immediately he sprang into action, drawing his gun as he took a dive to the corner. At that same moment, the girls also sprang into action as they cartwheeled to corners at the opposite side of the room.

"Uncle Frank don't shoot, it's Melissa!!!" she yelled

"The police informed me that my niece Melissa was dead, so who are you and what are you doing here?" he questioned from the corner.

"Uncle Frank it is truly me, Precious. I entered through our very own secret entrance because I had no one left. Everyone else is dead: Mom, Dad, and Jack." She knew that he would recognize the name Precious because only he called her by that name.

Slowly he emerged from the corner as she acknowledged the voice of the child he loved so dearly. "Precious, is that you?" as he came to her now with opened arms. "My child, I have mourned for your loss for so long! This is a miracle and the best gift I have had in a long time," hugging and kissing her.
"Uncle Frank, things have been so rough without my parents and John. Everyone is gone. No one is alive but you and I. I feel so alone." Melissa for the first time, entirely released all her frustration, anger, sadness, and loneliness on Uncle Frank. "I have been living on the streets for so long, but I never forgot you. I knew that I had to make it back to you," as she kept on crying hysterically.
Uncle Frank stroked her hair with affection. All of

his love for his long lost niece called Precious came flooding back. "You are safe now Precious. You are all grown up and beautiful. Let me take a look at you." He stepped back from Melissa as he looked at her with admiration. "You have grown into a gorgeous young lady and I am so proud of you. I missed you, my child. You brought extreme joy to my life, and I consider you my only daughter. When I heard that you were gone life was not the same from that time on."

Melissa hugged him again saying, "Uncle Frank, I love you."

"So much was taken from me when I discovered that you all were gone." I stay away from the house now because it holds so many terrible memories. I visit every six months to check on both your house and mine. Still deciding what I want to do with them." He looked down at his feet sadly then smiled at Melissa because this was truly a joyous moment to celebrate.

From the far corner, Samantha came, startling Uncle Frank. He began saying "Who, who....?"

"This is my friend Samantha," Melissa said as she introduced the girl who was as pretty as she but taller with red hair.
Uncle Frank smiled and stretched out his hands to greet her. "Welcome to my humble home," he said.

"Humble? It's incredible and it is a pleasure

to meet you finally," Samantha replied shaking Uncle Frank's hand happily.

"When did you get here? How long have you been here? What are your plans? Are you ok? Do you need some money and a place to stay? This city would not be the safest place for you right now because things are still rough with the Gonzales Drug Family," Uncle Frank said, all in one breath.

"I am here to make them pay for what they did to my family," said Melissa angrily.

"WOW!" "WOW! Slow down now. That is a big job you are talking about and you are not prepared to take on the Drug Lords in this town. Not even the police are able to manage them. Since they killed your parents, they have executed several other drug enforcement officers and their families." Uncle Frank said with concern in his voice. "You came with what army to tackle such a mighty job?" he asked.

"Samantha and I have been training to fight them for months now, and we are excellent. I know that all we need is a little more time, and we will be ready, Will you help us?" she asked Uncle Frank, opening her lovely brown eyes, pouting her lips, and batting her lashes like she did many years ago and it worked all the time.

"Don't give me that face young lady. It will not work this time. Taking down that crime family is a dangerous job for you to undertake. I will not lose you twice. I have you now and I will keep you safe."

"Uncle Frank, if they ever know that I am alive they will hunt me down and kill me. So I have no life right now. They have to pay for killing my family and if you don't help us, we will do it alone."

"Ok. Let me see what you got. Convince me that you are serious and prepared for battle," he said with amusement.

Right then, the girls sprang into action somersaulting into combat position as they took down Uncle Frank with their surprise attack. He hit the floor hard while they made their escape silently.

Uncle Frank stood up surprised and a little shaken by the sudden attack of the girls as he looked for them. They came at him again. This time once again pinning him to the floor now as he begged for their mercy. "STOP!!!! STOP!!!!" he yelled. "You have proved your point. "Where and when did you learn to fight like that?"

"We have been training in your secret room," Melissa said

"What secret place?" pretending he did not know what she meant and wondering how she found it.

"The one behind the bookshelf."

"How do you know about that room?"

I found it by mistake one night when I was

55

looking for a book to read. I was so young when I saw you doing some amazing things. I continued looking at you while you were training yourself. I started to go in the room by myself practicing what I saw you do for years, Uncle Frank."

Uncle Frank scolded her "that was sneaky. My child, you could have hurt yourself," He was proud to see how she had grown up to be amazing like her parents. They were magnificent he thought to himself. No one had ever been able to take him down like that. This task might be possible. With a little more training they would be ready to combat the Drug Lords. He included himself in the group to make sure that they stay alive.

He scolded them by saying "This is not child's play. These are terrible men and you should not think that they will willingly allow you to defeat them. They have big guns, knives, and sophisticated weapons prepared and waiting for whoever believes that they can fight them."

"Yes we know that, but we will take them down with our strengths at their weakness. They won't know who or what hit them. Not even long after we have gone," Melissa said making a fist.

'We have to map out a careful plan how to do this. We have to strategize every second, of every minute, of every day that we attack." Uncle Frank said aloud.

"Uncle Frank, did you say we? Are you going to

help us get those evil men that hurt our families?"

"Yes child, I lost you once. I will not let you go against the Drug Lords by yourself. We will come up with a plan, but how we execute that plan will determine the success of our Revenge Plot." Come, girls. We have plenty of work to do."

And so they moved into the secret room. The girls filled Uncle Frank in on all that had happened to them, their hardship, misfortunes, and sleepless nights on the streets and their quest for revenge.

Uncle Frank, Melissa, and Samantha

Chapter 9

THE PLOT

With a plan firmly in place, Uncle Frank, Samantha and Melissa started on their mission to take down the Gonzales Drug family. They embarked upon the police station. Samantha was assigned to be the distraction. She had to cause a diversion to the security guards so that Melissa could go in to do her part. Samantha distracted them with her best-distracting move. She called it her "you can't stop this hot girl move." In other words, she was flirting with them. Melissa saw that it was time for her to sneak inside the police station she snuck in and sprayed the surveillance cameras.

Uncle Frank wore a black mask with a black jumpsuit. As for Samantha, she wore a beautiful wig dressed as a super model. Melissa took out the cameras and climbed into the vent putting sleeping gas in front of all the fans inside the vent for it to enter the building. A few minutes passed, and all the police officers fell asleep except the guards that Samantha was distracting.

Melissa was finished with her task and came out of the vent. As she exited, she changed her clothing and signaled to Samantha that she had completed her job. Samantha had to make her departure, so she quickly ended the conversation saying

"I have to get going."

"Ok," said the officer.

"Bye," Samantha said as she walked out the door. I will come back later to talk some more."

At that point, it was time for Uncle Frank to do his part. He took a laser, cut a hole in the ceiling and lowered himself into the room with a grappling hook. He took pictures of the evidence from the police files of the crime scene involving the murder of his brother and his wife.

Now they were ready. The three warriors had the evidence, training, and weapons. All they needed now was a good plan. Uncle Frank had so many gadgets and guns and about one year to make sure that they had all bases covered.

60

Now that they had all the proof they needed to bring justice for their families, it was time to make up a good plan of action. They would call it Sweet Revenge or SR Plot which they broke into three sections.

Month 1

Identify the Drug Lords responsible for the murders and study their strengths, weaknesses, and patterns of operation.

From the evidence they had in hand, they could recognize each and every member of the Gonzales Drug Family guilty of the crime.

Follow them. Find out where they lived, played, and operated their business.

First three months

With the evidence in hand, follow the drug family. Gather vital information such as where they lived, time the movements of family members, security guards and of course, Papa, the head of the Gonzales Drug Family and his daily routine.

Papa was a huge hairy Spanish man with plenty fat to share. He was a character who commanded much attention, gave many orders to all around him and demanded loyalty to his family.

His eldest twin sons Jose and Paco were also overweight. Their skin shone, and they dressed casually, but you could see that their clothes were very expensive. We observed that the middle son Roberto, was smaller and was always well dressed in the finest Italian suits but he looked as if Paco and Jose ate all his food. He looked a bit shy, but the ladies seemed to like him a lot.

They had many cousins, but Stephano and his brother Juan Carlo stuck out more prominent than the rest because they were as pretentious as Paco and Jose. He threw his money around, drove in limousines and took the same drugs they sold on the streets.

"This one can be the weak spot; we need to get to know him," Melissa said

"Does that mean we have to party?" asked Samantha.

"Yep," said Melissa smiling at her friend who was naturally excited about the thought of partying.

"We have to be careful and make sure we don't blow our cover."

It had been three months since they started investigating the suspects. Today there was a big meeting planned. All the heads of the family were supposed to participate. Most of them were on Melissa's list of suspects. The meeting was held at 8:00 pm in the darkness of the night at their favorite hotel. Security was tight from all angles: the roof, the doors, the lobby, and surrounding the building. No ordinary person could penetrate this operation.

"We have our work cut out for us here. This revenge is not an easy job," Samantha said.

"Yes, we are up against an organized drug and crime family, so their security is tight. We have the element of surprise, so we can do it."

"Two cute Ninja warriors," she said with a grin.

"We have still some preparations to do so let's go home," Melissa said as they faded into the darkness.

From the information gathered they knew that the job was harder than they expected. Preparations were minutely detailed now to get them ready to do what seemed to be the impossible. The girls never did anything like this before but were excited for the challenge knowing that one wrong move could cost them their lives.

Second 3 months

Uncle Frank, Melissa and Samantha still following the drug family learning the patterns of movements and how they moved about their daily lives. They had to step up their operation now by getting inside the hotel called Paco's Place where their meetings were held.

Melissa got a job as a custodian for the 8th floor, so she studied the layout of the site, moving about on elevators, going to the ceiling for cigarette breaks, but she did not smoke. This break allowed her to assess the possibilities of them entering through the roof. She studied the cameras in place, the guards, and every detail of the structure.

Melissa would let Uncle Frank in on occasions with a uniform she took from the uniform supply room so he could get an accurate design for their virtual projection for practicing. Samantha and Melissa visited the club at the hotel where the Gonzales Drug Family loved to relax and play.

Melissa disguised as Sara in the hotel was invited because she was now known by the Drug Family to be a beautiful, friendly worker who loved to party.

"Hello Stephano! Nice seeing you here tonight. Remember to save me a dance." Melissa said. Her blood was boiling because she could not stand being around the people who killed her and Samantha's family.

"Absolutely Sara! Come over and party with me tonight, ok?" Stephano said.

"Let me introduce you to my girlfriend Wendy," as she pointed to Samantha, who was dressed as beautiful as she was.

"Wow! Double trouble! Come over and party with us." He led the beautifully dressed ladies to his table.

Stephano and Juan Carlos were drunk a lot, smoked cigars, and used the same drugs they were destroying the city with. How stupid could they be? When they were high, you could get any information from them. After about 2 hours of partying Melissa asked Stephano "Hey man, when is the next big meeting? You can invite me as your girlfriend," she said cunningly.

"Sara, I like how you think, it's every three months, and you can come with me to the next one." Stephano too drunk or high to know that the information he revealed was supposed to be confidential.

The ladies left the hotel with vital information confirming that they had a set pattern in place. Uncle Frank created the virtual layout of the building; especially the 8th floor where they would have their sweet revenge.

Final 3 months

It was now seven months into the operation and time to secure the plot and prepare to execute it. Training was now very intense for the ladies who were now more determined to succeed at this mission. Uncle Frank would leave them to practice while he went out to take care of what he called significant business. They did not mind him being away because it allowed them to continue practicing and collected all the remaining supplies to get the job done. Their dedication to the plan made Uncle Frank more confident than ever that the little girl he loved so dearly was now grown up and fiercer than her mother whom he once trained.

"I am so proud of you both. You have proven that you can accomplish this mission. Don't drop your guard for anything because they will be prepared to kill us at any moment if they suspect that we are onto them. For this last three months, I want you to fall back a little, so they don't suspect anything, especially coming to the day of the family meeting."

Time went by and it was finally five days less to complete the year. One day, Stephano approached Melissa saying, "Sara are you still interested in coming to the meeting as my girlfriend?"

Melissa was surprised that he remembered, and was also concerned if he knew who she was? For a second she felt that he wanted to trick her. "I would have loved to, but you never got back to me. I made plans with my cousin out of town, so I have to travel. That reminds me you think that I could get the weekend off to visit my family?" she asked batting her eyes.

"Sure, who could say no to that beautiful face? Make sure you cover your shift and enjoy your weekend."

"Yeah!!!" Melissa jumped pretending to be very excited. "The next time I see you, you would be dead," she muttered as she walked off in the opposite direction.

She told Uncle Frank what happened that

day, and he told her that it might not be any concern, but that means that they had to be extremely careful with a couple of days to "Mission Sweet Revenge."

Last remaining son comes in the room to find
everyone dead

Chapter 10

SWEET REVENGE

With the plot firmly in place Melissa, Samantha, and Uncle Frank set off to seek "Sweet Revenge (SR)" on the Gonzales Drug Family and do what the police had been trying to do for years; take them down like they have done to so many drug enforcement officers. The country had lost many innocent lives, and none of them had ever paid until now.

Before setting off, they went through the plan once more making sure that their exit plans were firmly in place.

Uncle Frank, "Code names Uncle Frank aka SR1, Melissa aka SR 2, Samantha aka SR 3 in position and ready to go?"

Uncle Frank, Melissa, and Samantha all said: "Check."

Uncle Frank began his checklist: "Everyone on location and arriving for the meeting?"
Melissa, "Check."

Uncle Frank, "Getaway car in location, keys in place?" Samantha, "Check.":

Uncle Frank, "all weapons, backup weapons, still pictures for cameras, ammunition, a bulletproof vest?"

Melissa, "Check."

Uncle Frank, "Flashlights, gadgets, all wired correctly and communications clear, backup tickets, passports, and id in place?"

Samantha "Check, testing, testing, testing."

Uncle Frank, "All watches synchronized and ready to go?"

Both girls said, "Check!" It was now 5:00 pm and all was ready for operation Sweet Revenge.

They walked about a quarter mile down the road together and flagged down a taxi making sure that their drop off point was two blocks away from the action point. Each person took different directions but meeting at Paco's Place at three corners of the building Uncle Frank located at the head of the corner, and the two girls on either end North and West. He made his signal and they moved in.

Melissa shot the grappling hook to the top of the building once no one was in sight and lifted herself to the upper part of the building. Locating Target 1, she hit him in the neck with a poisoned dart gun muttering, "SR2 in position and target is down."

Samantha entered the building from the far right and took the elevator to the 8th floor then began to walk towards the conference room, "SR

3 in position and target two is in sight."

Uncle Frank walked forward into the building and took the elevator straight ahead of him taking it to the 8th floor, "SR 1 in position and walking in your direction and target 3 is in sight."

As they advanced to the meeting room, they replaced still pictures of the room so no one would suspect that their operation was in progress.

Melissa was making her way down the stairs from the top of the building to target 4, "Target 4 is in sight and preparing to attack. KA WACK, mark four down and moving towards you."

Everyone replied heading into position. "Two down the hall and heading in."

They entered the meeting room now, and all prime targets were in place with one the junior son missing but no time to waste. They flooded the room with tear gas from every direction stunning everyone. People started to run in every direction. With SR1, SR2, and SR3positioned at every exit it was easy to kill everyone as they left the room panicked and confused. With all the lookout guards taken out early, no one was on the outside to hinder their mission.

"Who are you and what are you doing here? One tall, man dressed in combat uniform asked Samantha.

"You don't know me hombre?" as she stepped back the man knocked her to the ground.

Samantha, "I'm down, needing cover."

Uncle Frank ran to her assistance, so this left his exit opened for things to go wrong and it did. Things turned around and the Drug Lords turned to fire on them. Melissa, sensing that things were about to go terribly wrong, managed to maneuver from her end killing, all in her path as she tried to tidy up the mission. She got to her Uncle Frank and Samantha, who were now under fire from the Drug Lords. With three people now fighting against the crime family operation, Sweet Revenge managed to get control of the situation and put the backup plan into effect.

"Get up Samantha, are you all right?" He asked her as she held her bruised shoulder.

"Yes.., He came from behind and startled me," Samantha said with disappointment in her voice.

"Let's go," Uncle Frank said sharply yet happy that she was all right.

Just then, a huge man came from nowhere and appeared in the doorway which was foggy from their smoke bombs. The man pointed a gun at them and motioned them back into the room. They backed up slowly as he came towards them. As they entered into the light, the man exclaimed and said: "Uncle Frank, so this is how you repay us? How could you betray us like this?" Right, then the man pulled the trigger towards them. Uncle Frank went for his legs shouting "RUN!!!" Samantha and I dove into the corner and made our way to the door. Uncle Frank overpowered him and shot him with the gun he once pointed at us.

While we made our way down the stairs, Uncle Frank called the police precinct to put phase three in motion. I could not help wondering who that man was, and why he called him Uncle Frank.

Phase three was now in place and the Police precinct called to come in on the back end to clean up the mess. They set off the fire alarm and exited with the crowd. To their surprise, the missing son was entering at the same time as the crowd was leaving. Melissa bumped into him as she ran for safety.

She yelled, "Sorry, sorry," as she ran for cover.

"I hope you are fine?" noticing how pretty she was.

"What is going on in here and where is everyone?" check on Papa and make sure he gets out of here," he pointed to his security as he hurried upstairs ahead of him. Juan tried to manage the crown in the midst of the panic then made his way to the 8th floor. What he saw made him drop to his knees. The entire family was shot dead.

He saw his father slumped over a chair taking his last breath, Papa don't leave me, who did this? Papa don't die." He hugged his father in his arms and cradled him until the police arrived with guns drawn.

The chief constable was present and sized up the situation and said in a loud voice, "No one move, help is on the way." The sight of the Gonzales Drug Family lying dead pleased his heart, for now, he could rest safer at night.

He looked at Juan warning him that he would come and get him personally if he was to hear about any retaliation. "Take time and bury your dead and keep the peace or we will charge you. I would get out of town if I were you because everyone who has been ever gunning for your family will be after you now. Papa is dead, and the turf belongs to anyone now."

Juan shook his head in agreement now knowing that the Police Chief was right. "You are right."

"I don't know who did this, but we thank them because they did what we could not do." The Chief walked off with a smile on his face knowing that things would be a little quiet for some months to come, even though disputes would be taking place for ownership of the Gonzales Drug Families' turf. Uncle Frank escaped separately but making sure that Melissa and Samantha were safe and in the waiting vehicle.

"Goodbye, for now, I love you," Melissa said as Uncle Frank kissed them on the cheek.

"Love you too, and great job. I will try to visit sometime."

The girls were speeding to the airport now in

silence. Samantha was rubbing her bruised shoulder but feeling fine. They arrived at the airport parked the rental car and changed their clothing into new disguises. They dumped their clothing in a garbage can a distance from the parked car and made their way to their flight.

"Announcing flight 953 to France now boarding!!!" The girls made their way to check in because they booked earlier in the day to save time. They checked in and went their way on the airplane. They sat in separate seats all the way to France.

All alone in her place, Melissa began to reflect on the events of the day. However, the most memorable were the incident with that man who almost killed them. The words, 'Uncle Frank, how could you betray us like this?' haunted her. She had so many questions but no answers. She wondered if Uncle Frank was part of the drug family. Was he part of a rival drug family? Was this revenge about his personal revenge or about avenging the death of her family? Just then, she remembered what her mother had told her that Uncle Frank was once a very dangerous man. Was he a Drug Lord like the Gonzales family? She began to put some events together wondering where Uncle Frank went to every day while they were practicing. How did he know so many personal details about the Gonzales family, and was he once part of them?" This conflicting information was becoming very disturbing to Melissa as she faded into a sleep tired from months or training, and now the closure that she was looking for was now filled with doubts and questions.

They finally arrived in France but took separate taxis to the house assigned to them. When they got there, they were surprised to see the fantastic house they would call home for as long as they needed it.

"This was both, the most frightening, happy, and confusing day of my life," said Melissa.

"I agree with you Melissa; I am delighted that we finally have our sweet task revenge accomplished," replied Samantha.

Melissa did not voice her suspicion about Uncle Frank being a double agent working for them and someone else. And that he had other motives for killing the Gonzales family other than their revenge.

"Revenge was sweet. Now I can go on with my life. France is going to be great," Samantha said. Melissa shook her head and said, "We'll see, let us remain alerted while we enjoy our new life." They walked off together to see France and all the promise it had for them.

More books to come

ABOUT THE AUTHOR

Khayah Daniella Browne is a strong-willed determined child. She was born in 2003 on St. Croix United States Virgin Island with rough beginnings but grew up to be an inspiration. Her will to survive and her dedication to try new things is astonishing. She loves dancing, reading, writing, singing, playing her violin, and challenging any sporting activity. She has aspirations to one day become a lawyer and a gymnast.

www.ingramcontent.com/pod-product-compliance
Lightning Source LLC
Chambersburg PA
CBHW072018170626
46813CB00005B/2181